AlphaBest

To Andrew, Andrewer, Andrewest — H.B.

For my wonderful wife, Carla — D.W.

Kids Can Press acknowledges the financial support of the Government of Ontario, through the Ontario Media Development Corporation's Ontario Book Initiative; the Ontario Arts Council; the Canada Council for the Arts; and the Government of Canada, through the BPIDP, for our publishing activity.

Published in Canada by
Kids Can Press Ltd.
25 Dockside Drive
Toronto, ON M5A 0B5

Published in the U.S. by
Kids Can Press Ltd.
2250 Military Road
Tonawanda, NY 14150

www.kidscanpress.com

The artwork in this book was rendered in ink and watercolor.
The text is set in GrilledCheese BTN.

Edited by Karen Li
Designed by Marie Bartholomew

This book is smyth sewn casebound.
Manufactured in China, in 4/2012, through Asia Pacific Offset, 3/F, New factory (No.12), Jing Yi Industrial Center, Tian Bei Estate, Fu Ming Community, GuanLan, Bao An, Shenzhen, China

CM 12 0 9 8 7 6 5 4 3 2 1

Library and Archives Canada Cataloguing in Publication

Becker, Helaine, 1961–
    Alphabest : the zany, zanier, zaniest book about comparatives and superlatives / written by Helaine Becker ; illustrated by Dave Whamond.

ISBN 978-1-55453-715-0

1. English language — Comparison — Juvenile literature.
2. English language — Adjective — Juvenile literature.
I. Whamond, Dave II. Title.

PE1241.B43 2012   j425.5   C2012-900997-0

Kids Can Press is a *corus*™ Entertainment company

AlphaBest

The Zany, Zanier, Zaniest Book about Comparatives and Superlatives

Written by Helaine Becker

Illustrated by Dave Whamond

Kids Can Press

Most Magnificent

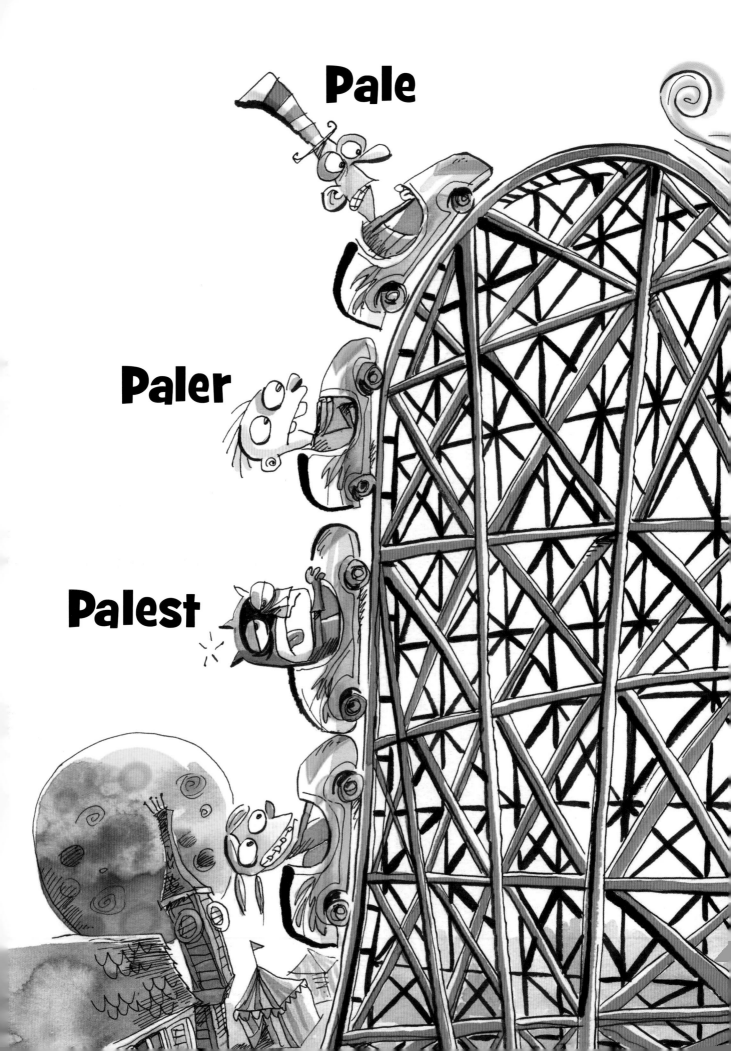

Quick

Quicker

Quickest

Unique

eXtra
large

eXtra
EXTRA
large

eXtra
eXtra
EXTRA
large

Zany

Good, Better, Best!

Teaching Kids to Form Comparatives and Superlatives

From an early age, children learn to use adjectives to describe the world. *Funny, giant, red* and *lemony* are all adjectives. So are all the words pictured in this book. How many more adjectives can your kids think of?
Comparative adjectives are used to compare two objects. Say, for example, you have two apples. How do you tell them apart? It would be easy if the apples had different qualities, such as if one were red and the other green. But what if they were both red? After reading this book, children will likely be able to form comparatives by intuition. Even so, here are the rules, just in case they ask!

To form the comparative, add the ending *–er* to the main adjective to create a new word. You can start with the adjective *round*. Simply add the *–er* ending to make the word *rounder*. Now you can compare apples to apples: "My apple is *rounder*."

TEACHING TIP
Comparative adjectives are followed by the word "than" when a comparison is made between objects; for example, "My apple is rounder than your apple."

Sometimes when you compare two objects, such as our round apples, it's not enough to say one is rounder than the other. What if one of those apples is actually rounder than every other apple?

If so, we use another kind of adjective called a superlative adjective.

To form the superlative, add the ending *–est* to the main adjective. Now you can describe your own, super-wonderful apple: "My apple is the *roundest* of all apples."

TEACHING TIP
Superlative adjectives are normally preceded by the word "the."

Adjective	Comparative	Superlative
round	round**er**	round**est**
loud	loud**er**	loud**est**

Some words use a slightly different pattern.

When a short word (such as *hot, big* or *red*) ends in a consonant, double the final consonant before you add the *–er* or *–est* endings.

Adjective	Comparative	Superlative
hot	hot**ter**	hot**test**
thin	thin**ner**	thin**nest**

When the word ends in **e**, such as *pale* or *gentle*, just add *–r* for the comparative and *–st* for the superlative.

Adjective	Comparative	Superlative
pale	pale**r**	pale**st**
brave	brave**r**	brave**st**

If the word ends in a *y*, such as *icy* or *angry*, change the *y* to an *i*, then add the standard endings (*–er* and *–est*) to form the comparative or superlative.

Adjective	Comparative	Superlative
greedy	greedi**er**	greedi**est**
funny	funni**er**	funni**est**

Most long words use helper words, such as *more* and *most*, before the adjective to form the comparative and superlative.

Adjective	Comparative	Superlative
magnificent	*more* magnificent	*most* magnificent
frightening	*more* frightening	*most* frightening

TEACHING TIP
Less **and** ***least*** **are the opposite of** ***more*** **and** ***most***; **for example, "My costume is** ***less*** **frightening than yours. My costume is the** ***least*** **frightening of all."**

Some words don't follow any rules! We just have to memorize these. Here are the most common rule-breakers.

Adjective	Comparative	Superlative
good	better	best
bad	worse	worst
far	farther	farthest
many	more	most